THIS

SWEET PICKLES ®

BOOK
BELONGS TO

_____

In the world of *Sweet Pickles,* each animal
gets into a pickle because of an all too human
personality trait.

This book is about Jealous Jackal who is
convinced that everyone else is better off
than he is.

Books in the Sweet Pickles Series

Library of Congress Cataloging in Publication Data

Reinach, Jacquelyn.
  Jackal wants everything.

  (Sweet Pickles series)
  SUMMARY: Jackal wants everything he sees—and then
some more.
  [1. Jackals—Fiction] I. Hefter, Richard.
II. Title. III. Series.
PZ7.R2747Jac   [E]   77-16324
ISBN 0-03-042036-5

Printed in the United States of America

Weekly Reader Books' Edition

Weekly Reader Books presents

JACKAL
WANTS
EVERYTHING

Written by Jacquelyn Reinach
Illustrated by Richard Hefter
Edited by Ruth Lerner Perle

Holt, Rinehart and Winston · New York

Jackal was bicycling up Fourth Street one afternoon when he saw a lot of cars parked in front of Zebra's house. Then he heard a lot of laughing and singing coming from the yard.

He chained his bike to a tree and went to see what was going on.

It looked like Zebra was having a party. And everyone else was there.

Jackal felt hot. Then he felt cold. Then he bit his lip. Then he gnashed his teeth and scowled.

Zebra saw Jackal and waved. "Oh, there you are, Jackal. Come on in."

"You're having a party!" whined Jackal. "Why wasn't I invited?"

"You *are* invited!" chuckled Zebra. "Everybody's *always* invited to my parties."

"Well, I certainly didn't get an invitation!" grumbled Jackal.

"That's because I didn't send any," said Zebra. "I never send invitations. I figured everybody would hear about it sooner or later."

"Yes!" called Alligator. "I heard about it from Yak."
"I heard it from Alligator," said Dog.
"I heard it from Dog," squealed Nightingale.
"A little bird told me," joked Kangaroo.

Jackal felt cold. Then he felt hot. Then he gnashed his teeth and yelled, "No fair! Everybody told everyone but me! You all know I work all day. Nobody ever tells me anything. I don't have any friends. I never hear what's going on!"

"There's a party going on," smiled Zebra. "Why don't you come in and have a good time?"

Jackal took a step back. "I know when I'm not wanted," he said. "Anyway, you didn't even tell me the reason for the party."

"I'M the reason!" called Moose happily. "Isn't it wonderful? Zebra's giving this beautiful party just for me!"

"Hooray!" yelled everybody.

Jackal felt hot and cold at the same time. Then he bit his lip and gnashed his teeth and marched right up to Zebra.

"Why are you giving a party for *Moose*?" he demanded. "Why don't you give a party for *me*? It's not fair. I WANT A PARTY! I deserve a party more than Moose."

Moose burst into tears. "That's a terrible thing to say," he sobbed. "Now you've spoiled my beautiful party!"

"So what?" sniffed Jackal. "Why should you be the one who always gets everything?"

"But this is the first party I've ever had!" cried Moose.

"Well, I never had a party either!" yelled Jackal. "IT'S NOT FAIR!"

Elephant stepped between them and smiled. "Break it up, guys!" she said. "Wouldn't you rather eat than fight? There's a lot of delicious cake left!"

"Yes," laughed Kangaroo. "Take a cake break. Haw, haw!"

Suddenly Moose began to laugh, too. "Of course," he giggled. He threw his arm around Jackal and said, "Come on, pal. Let's have some cake!"
Elephant started to cut the cake for Moose and Jackal.

Jackal watched as she cut two slices. Then he pulled a ruler out of his pocket and began to measure each slice. He measured top to bottom, front to back, and side to side.

Then Jackal sniffled and whined and cried, "No fair! No fair! Moose's piece is bigger than mine! I want it! I want it! I want it!"

Jackal jumped up and down and fell SPLAT, right on top of the cake.

Zebra handed a towel to Jackal and said,"Having fun?"

"It's no fair!" sniffled Jackal, wiping his face. "I only want what's coming to me. You're all so *mean*!"

"Why don't you stop being so weird?" yelled Alligator.

"He can't help it," said Lion. "He gets jealous."

"Jealous? Who's jealous?" snapped Jackal. "I'm not jealous. There isn't a jealous bone in my whole body!"

"Oh, no!" giggled Kangaroo. "Jackal isn't jealous. All he wants is a written invitation. All he wants is a party of his own. All he wants is more cake. All he wants is *everything*!"

Everybody giggled.

"Boy, this is a dumb party!" sniffed Jackal. "And you're all picking on me!" He started kicking the table. "Who wants to be at a party like this, anyway?"

"Watch out!" cried Walrus. "The table's wobbling!" Jackal gave another big kick and ran off. The table fell over.

"Ooooh!" screamed Nightingale. "We should really get him for that!"

"Yes!" said Zebra. "And I know how."

"How?" cried everybody.

"We should really get him..." said Zebra, "to stop being so jealous. I think that if *just once* we gave Jackal everything he wants, he wouldn't feel so jealous."

"I get it!" cried Dog. "And if he doesn't feel so jealous, maybe Jackal won't be such a pain!"

"Good!" cried everybody. "Let's give Jackal everything he wants!"

They started to make plans.

The next afternoon, everybody went over to the gas station where Jackal worked. They were carrying balloons and banners, party hats and presents.

Pig handed Jackal a written invitation.

It said: THIS IS A SURPRISE PARTY FOR YOU, JACKAL. WE WANT TO GIVE YOU EVERYTHING YOU WANT!

"A surprise party for me!" said Jackal. "Is this a trick? You know I'm working now. How can I have a party when I'm working?"

"Easy," said Zebra. "Since everybody in town wants to give you a party, then nobody will want to buy gas. You won't have to work, and we can have fun instead."

"Hooray!" cried everybody. And the party began. There was laughing and music and a pile of presents for Jackal.

Elephant's present was a year's supply of chocolate layer cake with banana frosting. Hippo brought Jackal a book called SOYBEANS AND FRIENDSHIP. Lion's present was an afternoon at the movies—just the two of them. Yak's present was to call Jackal every night for a month and tell him what was going on.

"Well, Jackal," laughed Zebra, "*now* we hope you have everything you want!"

"Yes," said Yak. "We stayed at Zebra's house and planned your party all night. And we worked to make decorations, and we made hats and blew up the balloons, and Elephant did all the cooking. What more could anyone want…?"

Jackal felt hot. Then he felt cold. Then he bit his lip. Then he gnashed his teeth and screamed, "What more? What more? I'll tell you what more! You always leave me out of all the fun! You guys were up all night having a good time together. Without me! NO FAIR!"

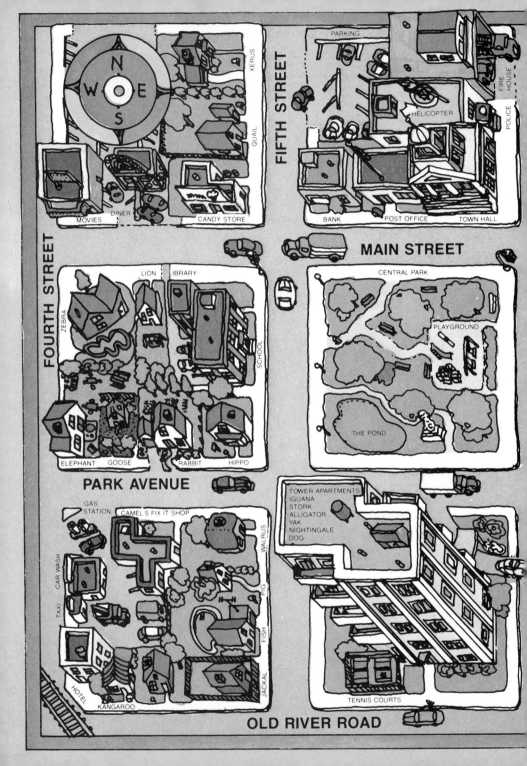